**Parents and Children
Look at Problems Together**

SYCAMORE STORIES

Stories by

Jerome R. Koch

Fortress Press   Philadelphia

SYCAMORE STORIES
Parents and Children Look at Problems Together

Edited by Linda Schomaker.
Designed and illustrated by Jim Stewart.

Library of Congress Cataloging-in-Publication Data

Koch, Jerome R.
  Sycamore stories.

  Bibliography: p.
  Contents: Starting Sunday school—Accidents
sometimes happen—Bo loses his job—[etc.]
    [1. Dogs—Fiction. 2. Christian life—Fiction]
  I. Title.
PZ7.K789Sy 1986   [Fic]   86-9828
ISBN 0-8006-1945-5

2104C86   Printed in U.S.A.   1–1945

CONTENTS

Foreword

Most young children love to be read to. This book was designed for adults and children to read together. The issues dealt with will undoubtedly cause children to ask questions. Therefore, if an adult is reading the book with the child, there will always be someone there to listen to the child's questions and comments. That's not to say that the adult will have the answers to all of those questions! When children feel secure enough to ask questions, and when adults take the time to listen to those questions and answer them as best as they are able, feelings of security and trust develop. This kind of relationship building can be a happy side effect of enjoying this book.

At the end of each story I have added a brief section entitled "Notes," which includes some thoughts about how you as an adult might help the child deal with the problem raised in the story. In addition, at the end of the book you will find an annotated bibliography of children's books that deal with the same issues. If you and the child want to explore the issues further, reading and talking about these additional books would be a way to begin. Most of them are available at your public library or can be obtained at a local bookstore.

An underlying theme for all of the stories is prayer. Children and adults alike can find comfort in prayer. Take advantage of Sycamore's folding his paws and praying to help the child to whom you are reading this book develop his or her ability to find comfort in prayer.

Linda Schomaker

Preface

This book is about Sycamore the puppy. The stories confront common life issues and are written to be read to children aged three through eight. Some older children who read at about a fourth-grade level may enjoy reading about Sycamore themselves.

Though Sycamore is a puppy, he lives in a human world and interacts with children and adults as though he were human. This enables him to encounter real-life situations which children can relate to. Yet because he is a puppy, his problems can remain safely distant from the children when necessary.

As Sycamore encounters the joy and pain that life can bring, he finds ways to persevere and grow. He becomes a kind of role model as the reader befriends him. This is not a "how to" book, however. Sycamore offers no recipes for dealing with life. Rather, it is a "how it is" book. I have tried to make these stories as realistic as possible, which means they have no pat answers or clichéd conclusions. To do that to such issues as unemployment, prejudice, friendship, hospitalization, and divorce compromises what even children know to be true.

Life is ambiguous, and the best we can do is make our way through it in the company of others and with an understanding of a God who walks with us also. Sycamore tries to be the kind of friend with whom that is possible. He asks good questions, and he learns that there are times when it feels right to fold his paws to pray.

I hope you enjoy getting to know my friend, Sycamore.

Jerome R. Koch

Starting Sunday School

Sycamore could stay in bed no longer. He had been awake for almost an hour, and it was only ten minutes to six. Since it was Sunday, he knew he shouldn't make too much noise this early, but today was a big day.

Sycamore's friend Pastor Paul had invited him to come to Sunday school. That was something Sycamore didn't know very much about. He had been to obedience school and learned to be a very well-mannered little puppy. And, like everyone else his age, soon he would go to kindergarten. But Sunday school? Sycamore was nervous. Pastor Paul's church was such a big place!

Sycamore had been to Trinity Church before with his parents, and he had met some of the boys and girls who came there each week. They all seemed quite nice. Sycamore especially liked it when one of the children scratched behind his ears. He wondered if anyone would have time to do that at Sunday school. Perhaps scratching wouldn't be allowed.

Since he couldn't sleep, Sycamore decided to go downstairs and try to have a quiet breakfast. He didn't want to wake his mom and dad. In the kitchen Sycamore found his puppy biscuits and sat down to eat. He wondered who his Sunday school teacher would be. Would she like having a rather shaggy puppy in her class? What if his teacher was a man? Would Sycamore like that better? There were so many things to think about all at once.

Sycamore finished his breakfast and rinsed his dishes. He noticed that the sun was shining into the den, so he walked over and flopped down on the rug in front of the window. The sun felt nice and warm. Sycamore closed his eyes.

"Sycamore," a voice called gently from the kitchen. It was Charlotte, Sycamore's mom. "It's after nine o'clock, and Sunday school starts in twenty minutes."

Sycamore quickly jumped up. He realized he had fallen back to sleep.

"You'll have plenty of time, Sycamore," Charlotte said. "It only takes ten minutes to walk to church, so go wash your face and brush your teeth."

As Sycamore ran upstairs, Charlotte thanked him for making his own breakfast and for cleaning up after himself. In a few minutes, he ran back down, scrubbed and ready to go.

"Your father has to go to work this morning," Charlotte said, meeting Sycamore at the door. "I'll come for you after Sunday school, and the two of us will go to church. Wait for me outside your classroom."

Just then Sycamore's dad, a big dog named Bo, came into the room. He was carrying a lunch pail and an envelope. Smiling, he said, "Don't forget your offering." He gave the envelope to Sycamore.

"Be careful crossing streets, and don't waste time sniffing fire hydrants," Charlotte said to the excited puppy. She patted his head and Sycamore was on his way.

He went straight to church. There was no time for dawdling and sniffing. As he turned the corner onto Campbell Street, Sycamore could see Pastor Paul greeting people as they left the building.

"Good," thought Sycamore. "The early service is just over." He knew he had enough time to get to Sunday school before class started.

"Sycamore, welcome!" It was Pastor Paul calling to Sycamore from the front of the church. "I've been waiting for you," he said. "I want to introduce you to your teacher. Mrs. Lewis is looking forward to meeting you."

"Maybe that means she likes puppies," thought Sycamore.

"You'll like getting to know Mrs. Lewis," said Pastor Paul. "She has three children, two cats, and a puppy of her own."

Sycamore wondered if Mrs. Lewis's cats scratched the nose of her puppy.

Pastor Paul motioned Sycamore toward the stairs. They got to class just as Mrs. Lewis was opening her songbook.

"Mrs. Lewis," said Pastor Paul, "I'd like you to meet Sycamore. He's the special friend of mine I was telling you about."

"Welcome, Sycamore! Come join us," said Mrs. Lewis. Sycamore thought she sounded friendly. He smiled. Mrs. Lewis continued: "Boys and girls, this is Sycamore. He's come to join our class."

Mrs. Lewis took Sycamore by the paw and led him toward a seat. One of the boys reached out to pet him, and Sycamore jumped. "Be gentle, Jimmy," said Mrs. Lewis. "You'll frighten him."

Sycamore was already a little frightened. A boy who looked like Jimmy had once pulled his tail.

Mrs. Lewis turned to Sycamore and said, "Jimmy has told us that puppies are his favorite animals."

Mrs. Lewis introduced Sycamore to the rest of the class. "That's Steven over by the window," she said, "and Jake is by the sink." Pointing to the children seated at the table, she said, "This is Charlene, C.J., Lara, Sara, Lisa, Nathan, Laurel, Chad, and Lindi." Sycamore hoped he could remember everyone's name since the children already knew his.

"We're getting ready to sing a song," said Mrs. Lewis. Everyone came over by the record player. Sycamore sat with them. Mrs. Lewis said, "The song is called 'If I Were a Butterfly.' "

It wasn't long before Sycamore forgot all about being nervous and shy. He liked to sing, and he enjoyed learning a song about butterflies, kangaroos, robins, and caterpillars. All the children seemed to want him for a friend. They colored flowers together and cut out a picture of Jesus. Sunday school was fun.

Very soon, it seemed, Sycamore heard a familiar voice say, "Are you having a good time?" Sycamore looked up. Pastor Paul was back. Sunday school was over and it was nearly time for church.

Sycamore was excited. "Yes," he said. "We learned about how much God loves everybody—boys, girls, elephants, and puppy dogs! He made us all special."

"Yes, he did," said Pastor Paul. "Knowing that makes us feel special and loved. Would all of you like to pray with me now and thank God for the way he loves us?" The children nodded, then finished putting away their crayons, paper, and scissors. They all sat down together.

"Sycamore, fold your paws," said Pastor Paul. "Let's pray. Dear God, thank you for new friends. Thank you for Sunday school, and for birds and puppies. Help us to remember that we all were made by you, and that you love us wherever we are. Amen."

Sycamore looked up. Everyone was smiling. He said good-bye to Mrs. Lewis and to all his new friends. He saw his mom at the door and ran to meet her.

NOTES: Starting Sunday school, though exciting for some children, will be scary for others. Young children usually feel more comfortable in new situations if they are told in advance a little about what to expect.

Begin to prepare the child for this new experience a few days before the first day of Sunday school. Give the child as much information as possible about what to expect, including who his or her teacher will be, what some of the activities will be, and where you will be while he or she is in Sunday school.

If possible, before the first day of school visit the room where the child will be attending Sunday school. Show the child where the bathroom is, and explain that you will come back to meet the child when Sunday school is over. Make your parting on the first day as matter-of-fact as possible, but be sensitive to your child's needs and stay nearby if he or she needs you.

Starting Sunday school is one more step towards independence for the young child. Be positive and supportive as he or she takes this step.

Accidents Sometimes Happen

Pastor Paul was worried. It was time for church to begin, and Sycamore had not arrived. What's more, Mrs. Lewis said he hadn't been to Sunday school either. That was very unusual. Sycamore hadn't missed Sunday school since he started coming over a month ago. Pastor Paul couldn't get Sycamore out of his mind as he got ready for worship.

When it came time in the service for the children's sermon, Pastor Paul tried to find out what was wrong. "Boys and girls," he said when they had come forward to sit with him, "I'm a little worried. Sycamore isn't here this morning and I don't know why. Have you seen him?" None of the children had. Pastor Paul continued, "I wonder if he's OK? He loves to come to church, and I don't understand why he's not here." All the children were concerned too. Sycamore was their friend and they missed him.

Since there didn't seem to be anything they could do at the moment, Pastor Paul, the children, and the congregation continued worship. Without Sycamore, however, it just wasn't the same.

When church was over, the boys and girls met Pastor Paul in his office. "Call Sycamore on the phone," they said. Gathering the children around him and closing the door, Pastor Paul did just that. He dialed Sycamore's phone number: 876–1553. After five rings, a familiar but very quiet voice answered.

"Hello?" It was Sycamore.

Pastor Paul was relieved. "Sycamore!" he exclaimed. "You're still at home! Did I wake you?"

"No," Sycamore said, "I've been up for a long time."

Pastor Paul was puzzled. "But Sycamore," he said, "you missed church and Sunday school. The boys and girls and I were worried about you. Are you sick?"

"No," said Sycamore, "I'm not sick. I'm, well, sort of afraid."

Pastor Paul wondered what Sycamore meant. "Afraid?" he said. "Afraid of what, Sycamore?"

Sycamore wasn't sure he wanted to say what it was he was afraid of. He was quiet for a moment; then he said, "Pastor Paul, I was afraid to come to church. I was afraid to come this morning because it's a Communion day."

It didn't seem to Pastor Paul that Sycamore was making any sense. "I don't understand, Sycamore," he said. "Why did Communion make you afraid today?"

Sycamore started to cry. Quietly he said, "I was afraid that if I came up to the Communion rail today, you might not bless me." The little puppy sniffed.

Now Pastor Paul was really confused. "That's silly, Sycamore. I always bless you when you come up to the Communion rail."

Sycamore sniffed again. "It's not silly, because I don't deserve to get blessed."

"So that's it," thought Pastor Paul. "Sycamore," he said gently, "tell me why you don't think you deserve a blessing."

Quietly Sycamore said, "My dad yelled at me last night."

Pastor Paul was listening. "Tell me more, Sycamore," he said.

"I chewed a hole in one of his favorite slippers by mistake," Sycamore said. "I thought it was an old sock. It smelled the same."

"That is sad," said Pastor Paul. "Did Bo spank you?"

"Yes," sniffed Sycamore, "and then I got so scared that I wet on the kitchen floor."

"That made it a lot worse, didn't it?"

"Yes. I slept outside all night."

Pastor Paul began to understand. "You made a mistake yesterday," he said, "so you're afraid that I might not bless you and that God might not love you anymore. Is that right?"

"Yes," said Sycamore, meekly.

"Sycamore," said Pastor Paul, "I have something very important to tell you. God knows all about yesterday and . . ."

"Does he hate me?" wailed Sycamore, interrupting.

"No, God doesn't hate you. God still loves all of us, even when we've been bad or made mistakes."

"Are you sure?" Sycamore wanted to know.

"Very sure," said Pastor Paul. "In fact, one of the things we remember on Communion days is that God forgives us. Always. Every time." Sycamore sniffed. "We miss you, Sycamore," said Pastor Paul. "We like it when you're here with us."

"I miss you, too."

"Are you still afraid?" asked Pastor Paul.

"Not so much," Sycamore answered.

Pastor Paul asked if Sycamore would be coming back to church next Sunday. "Even if I've been bad?" Sycamore wondered.

"Especially after you've been bad," said Pastor Paul. "We want you to know that we love you, and that God loves you, no matter what happens."

"I feel better," Sycamore said. "This week I'll be more careful."

"God bless you, Sycamore," said Pastor Paul.

Sycamore sniffed. "Thanks."

"All the boys and girls are here with me, Sycamore," said Pastor Paul. "Would you like to pray with us?"

"Yes," he said.

"Fold your paws then," said Pastor Paul. "Dear God, thank you. Thank you for loving us even on bad days. Help us remember how much you care for us so that we can stay away from trouble. Amen."

Sycamore said good-bye to Pastor Paul. As he hung up the phone, Sycamore began to smile.

NOTES: Forgiveness is a difficult concept for children to grasp. It is understandable that a young child has difficulty believing that God always loves him or her. One reason is that the child's knowledge of God and his works is so limited. Another reason is that the interaction he or she has had with those who are older causes the child to doubt that at certain times anybody loves him or her, let alone God.

If a child's parent yells as she or he drops and breaks a precious vase, doesn't it make sense that at that moment the child believes that the screaming parent does not love her or him? This parent, whom the child knows and loves so well, and who usually provides so much love and security for the child, has given the child reason to doubt that the love still exists. At a time when a child is learning trust, an outburst from someone dear to him or her can leave that child not only doubting the person's love, but also doubting God's love as well.

It is essential to the child's understanding of God's love to know that God will always love us, even when he doesn't love what we have done.

Bo Loses His Job

Sycamore took his time walking to Sunday school. It had been a very confusing week. Nothing like this had ever happened before. Sycamore felt alone and forgotten. It was even hard for him to pray. Sometimes it seemed that God just wasn't listening.

It had started to rain, but Sycamore didn't notice. He could only think about one thing. Maybe he could ask Mrs. Lewis about what had happened to him and his family. Surely Mrs. Lewis would be able to help a little. "Yes," he thought, "that's what I'll do."

When he got to his classroom, Sycamore sat down quietly, next to his friend Lindi. She scratched behind his ears and smiled. Then Mrs. Lewis came into the room. She started class by asking how everyone's week had gone. All the boys and girls said, "Fine!" Sycamore didn't say anything. He just raised his paw. Mrs. Lewis saw him and asked, "Do you have a question, Sycamore?"

Sycamore did. "Yes," he said. "Mrs. Lewis, does God . . ." Sycamore stopped. Now he wasn't sure if he should ask his question or not.

"Go ahead, Sycamore," said Mrs. Lewis.

Sycamore took a deep breath. "Mrs. Lewis," he said, "Mrs. Lewis, does God ever forget about us?"

Sycamore's teacher had not expected him to ask a question like that. Puzzled, she said, "No, Sycamore, God doesn't ever forget about us. Why do you ask?"

"I wondered," said Sycamore, "because it seemed last Friday like God forgot about my dad and our whole family."

Mrs. Lewis was curious, and suddenly very concerned. "What happened on Friday?"

Sycamore could feel his eyes starting to fill up. Quietly, he looked up and said, "Mrs. Lewis, on Friday my dad lost his job."

Everyone was quiet for a moment. Finally Mrs. Lewis said, "I'm sorry, Sycamore. That's really sad news. Can you tell us about it?"

"I don't understand it too well," Sycamore began. "My dad was a watchdog at the college. He worked most of the time in the boiler room. Last week his boss came and told him they didn't have enough money in the budget to keep paying a watchdog. He told my dad he couldn't work there anymore. I don't understand.''

Sycamore had to stop and wipe his eyes with his paw. He continued, ''He's a good watchdog too! One time there was a small leak in the furnace. Only my dad could smell it. He barked and barked until his boss came and found where the leak was. The man from the gas company said my dad might have saved the whole building from a big fire. I love my dad.'' Sycamore sniffed.

''Your dad is a very fine dog,'' Mrs. Lewis said. ''I'm sure he knows how much you love him. And, Sycamore, I want you to know that God loves Bo, and you, and your whole family very much too.''

Sycamore was confused. ''God loves us even if my dad isn't working anymore?'' he asked. ''We have to be really careful with our money now. And I just have a nickel for my offering. That's only half of what I usually give. Isn't God mad?''

''No, Sycamore,'' said Mrs. Lewis, ''I can't imagine that God is. God knows how sad you and your mom and dad are. Right now that's most important to God. I believe God is sad, too, when jobs are lost and families struggle. God knows that sad things happen—even to good watchdogs like Bo, and to good puppies like you. Believe me, Sycamore, God hasn't forgotten about you. God loves you very much. And God loves your mom and dad, too, especially on sad days.''

''Can we know that for sure?'' asked Sycamore.

''Yes,'' said Mrs. Lewis. ''The Bible says that nothing that happens to us can ever stop God from loving us. We also know from the Bible that God is with us wherever we go. God helps us through difficult days and weeks—even times like this for you and your family.''

''How does God do that?'' Sycamore wanted to know.

''When sad things happen,'' said Mrs. Lewis, ''God wants people like the boys and girls and me to take especially good care of you. We want you to tell us how we can help you and Bo and Charlotte now that Bo is no longer working. At the very least, we need to give you an extra hug today. Right now. That won't make trouble go away, but you'll know for sure that we love you very much. That's how you know God loves you, too, Sycamore. God helps all of us to be brave, and God asks us to trust him.''

Sycamore sniffed again. Mrs. Lewis said, ''Maybe now we should pray about this.''

''I'd like that,'' said Sycamore. ''I like hugs, too.''

16

"Fold your paws then," said Mrs. Lewis. "Let's pray. Dear Lord, it's a sad day for Sycamore and his family—especially for Bo. Help them to be brave. Help us care for them. Remind us all that you love us, even when we're sad. Amen."

Sycamore was crying softly. Everyone came over and gave him a hug, and Lindi scratched his ears again. As Mrs. Lewis opened her songbook, Sycamore began to feel a little less sad.

NOTES: When a parent loses his or her job, tremendous stress is placed on all members of the family. Parents can become so involved with their concerns about how they are going to make ends meet that they forget that the children in the family are also being affected by the change. It is important that the situation be explained to the child as simply as possible, the explanation, of course, being modified according to the age and ability of the child.

As adjustments in family routines and responsibilities are made, it is important that all children are made to feel that they are participating in these changes. For example, if certain cutbacks are going to have to be made, explain these changes to the child as simply as possible. Even very young children can be helped to understand that they will have to do without certain things because of the current situation.

Charlotte Goes Back to Work

It was a warm Wednesday afternoon. Sycamore was walking home from the grocery store, whistling to himself. His mom had sent him to get a large box of sandwich bags and some puppy biscuits. Since they were for him anyway, Sycamore was munching happily on one biscuit as he walked past Trinity Church. He noticed Pastor Paul's car in the parking lot and thought with a smile, "I've just got to tell him."

Sycamore went into the church building and found Pastor Paul reading at his desk. Pastor Paul looked up when he heard Sycamore knock on the door.

"Sycamore!" he exclaimed. "Come in and sit down." Pastor Paul poured himself another cup of coffee and got a bowl of water for Sycamore. "Tell me," he said. "What's new?"

Sycamore winked. "Want to hear some good news?" he asked.

"Sure," said Pastor Paul. "You have good news today?"

"Yes," said Sycamore. "Guess what happened yesterday afternoon!"

"I can't guess," said Pastor Paul. "What happened?"

"My mom came home late," said Sycamore. "My dad and I were outside playing. She said, 'Bo! Sycamore! Put the ball down and come inside. I want to talk to both of you.' We came in and sat at the kitchen table. Mom said, 'I have a surprise for you! I have the chance to go back to work!' "

"You chould have seen my dad's face. He was surprised all right! Before I was born, Mom worked at the firehouse. Even before my dad lost his job, I heard them talking about how much she missed her job. They told me they thought I was getting old enough to start taking more care of myself, especially since I'll be starting kindergarten soon. Anyway, yesterday Mom went and talked to her old boss. The fire chief told her they could really use a good fire dog. Then he offered her job back to her! She starts Monday. I'm real excited! So's my dad!"

"Are you sure about that?" asked Pastor Paul. "What did Bo say when he heard the news?"

"He didn't say anything right away," said Sycamore. "He sat and thought for a minute and was real quiet. Then he smiled and gave her a big hug."

"What terrific news!" exclaimed Pastor Paul. "What will your mom be doing at the firehouse?"

"That's the best part," Sycamore said, excitedly. "When she worked there before, all she did was make coffee and answer the phone. But do you know what she told the fire chief yesterday?"

"What did she tell him?" asked Pastor Paul.

"She said, 'If you really want me working here again, then I ride on the truck, just like any other fire dog!'"

Pastor Paul smiled. "Good for Charlotte," he said. "It's important for anyone who works to be treated fairly and with respect."

"That's what Mom always says," said Sycamore. "And even I know that moms are just as good as dads at barking and sniffing. My mom is a good fire dog. She's brave, too. I'm proud of her!"

"You should be," said Pastor Paul. "Charlotte is pretty special. With her working and Bo at home, there'll be changes around your house, won't there?"

"That's for sure," said Sycamore. "Starting next week, my dad's going to cook supper, and I get to help. I already know how to boil an egg. Three minutes seems like a long time when all you do is watch bubbling water. My dad's a special friend, and we're going to do lots of new things together—cooking, shopping, laundry, even cleaning. He told me we'd plant a garden real soon. I like tomatoes best."

"I'm very happy for you, Sycamore," said Pastor Paul. "It's great news about Charlotte and the firehouse, and you and your dad, too. Could we pray together about it?"

"I'd like that," said Sycamore.

"Fold your paws then," said Pastor Paul. "Dear God, thank you for good news. Help Charlotte with her new job at the firehouse, and help Sycamore and Bo get used to changes at home. Amen."

Sycamore looked up and smiled. Then Pastor Paul scratched him behind the ears.

NOTES: When mother goes to work there are many changes in the home. These changes should be explained to the child, and he or she should be made to feel part of new routines and responsibilities in the family. Just as Sycamore eagerly anticipated the many things he and Bo would be doing together, children can be helped to look forward to learning new skills and perhaps participating more fully in family tasks.

Remember that the child won't always be eager and happy about changes. It's not easy to give up familiar routines. Going to a baby-sitter after school or staying alone for a few hours isn't nearly as much fun as having mom waiting for you when you get home. It would be much nicer to go out and play with friends instead of doing chores. The reasons for the changes in routine will probably have to be explained many times, and the child's negative feelings about those changes should be accepted as valid. Listening to the child's concerns and feelings is an important aspect of the transition that takes place when mother returns to work.

Bo Starts School

Sycamore awoke with a start. He had been dreaming, and he was confused. He had dreamed he was walking home but couldn't remember where he lived. When he found a house that looked like his and went inside, all the furniture was rearranged, and the walls were painted the wrong colors. Shaking his head and blinking his eyes, Sycamore realized he was in his own bed and that he was safe inside his own home.

It was very early in the morning. The birds had just begun to sing. As he lay in bed, Sycamore thought about all the changes that had happened to him and his family. He had started Sunday school, and that was fun. Each week he learned more about how much God loved and cared for him. His teacher, Mrs. Lewis, and all the boys and girls in his class were good friends.

Sycamore remembered the day his dad had come home and told the family he'd lost his job. That had been a sad day. And there had been more sad days after that. Day after day Bo would come home from job-hunting, discouraged. Most of the places a watchdog might work had installed electronic security systems and no longer needed someone like Bo. Sycamore remembered how he had tried to cheer up his dad, and how much they enjoyed playing ball together.

About a month ago, Sycamore's mom surprised the whole family with her new job at the firehouse. Sycamore loved it when she would tell stories about the big red trucks, the siren, and the long fire pole the fire fighters slid down when the alarm sounded.

A week ago, Charlotte came home from the firehouse, tired and limping. There had been a big fire at a warehouse, and lots of people had come to watch the fire fighters put it out. Charlotte had to keep the crowd away by running back and forth in front of the burning building and barking. While she was doing that, part of the roof fell nearby, and some hot sparks singed her coat. Sometimes Sycamore worried about his mom getting badly hurt at work.

Things had changed around the house, too. Sycamore was quickly learning how much work it takes to keep a house running smoothly. He was responsible for making sure his dirty clothes got into the hamper. No one else had time to rummage through his closet. He and Bo went grocery shopping once a week. Together they planned a menu and made a list. Sycamore got to push the cart at the store and helped put the groceries on the checkout stand. Last week, part of Sycamore's fur got caught under the moving table that brought the groceries to the cash register. He had tried not to yelp too loudly, but almost everyone in the store heard him anyway. It hurt!

Suddenly Sycamore's alarm went off. He jumped and quickly shut it off. It was only 6:30! For a moment, Sycamore wondered why he had set it to ring an hour earlier than usual. Then he remembered. Today was another very special day, especially for dad.

Quietly, Sycamore got up and went downstairs. Opening the refrigerator, he took out mustard, lettuce, and an apple. In the cupboard he found lunch bags, potato chips, rye bread, and his dad's favorite—rawhide. In a few minutes, he had made what was sure to be a very tasty sandwich.

He put the sandwich, chips, and apple into a lunch bag; then, creeping quietly into the den, Sycamore found his crayons and a tablet of paper. Thinking hard and printing carefully, he wrote: "Love, Sycamore."

Sycamore put the crayons and tablet back into the desk where he had found them and took the note into the kitchen. He folded it carefully and put it inside the bag, along with his dad's lunch. Then, as quietly as he had come down, Sycamore went upstairs to his room and crawled into bed.

Snuggling under the covers, he thought about the afternoon last week when his dad had called him in from playing. Did Bo ever have a surprise for Sycamore! He had gone to the college to see his old boss, but he never made it to the boiler room. A sign on a bulletin board outside the Student Union caught his attention. It said, "SPECIAL OPPORTUNITY."

Bo stopped to read, and he learned about a class that would start just one week from that day—a class especially for big, strong, smart dogs. A teacher from Morristown, New Jersey, was coming to the college. He was going to stay for three months and train a class of guide dogs.

This was surely a special opportunity for Bo. He could learn to guide people who were blind and could not get around by themselves. Quickly Bo had read how and where to enroll and then

signed up for the course that very day. Today, one week later, Sycamore's dad was going to start school.

Sycamore felt warm inside after making his dad a surprise lunch. As he lay in bed, he closed his eyes and folded his paws. "Dear Lord," he prayed, "watch over my dad today. Help him learn how to be a good guide dog. He's a great dad and I love him. Bless us and, by the way, thanks. Amen."

A lot more changes were sure to come. Sycamore knew that. Through them all, God would guide and care for him and his family. Sycamore fell back to sleep, knowing that for sure.

NOTES: Many young children have never seen a guide dog and have no idea what purpose they serve. This story provides an opportunity to explain the function of these animals to the child.

Guide dogs are specially trained to assist people who can't see. The dogs wear a special harness which the blind person holds. The dog can then guide the person through traffic, on trains and buses, and anywhere else the person wants to go. Guide dogs are permitted by law to go everywhere with their person. These dogs open up a whole new world of opportunities for people who can't see.

Guide dogs usually live with families for the first year to eighteen months of their lives. They are then taken to a special school where they undergo rigorous training for their important job. When the dog is completely trained, he or she is given to a blind person who joins the dog at the school. The two are then trained together for another period of time to be sure they work well together as a team.

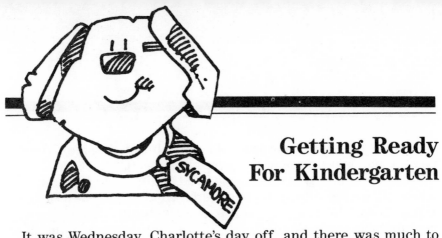

Getting Ready For Kindergarten

It was Wednesday, Charlotte's day off, and there was much to do. Sycamore had just finished rinsing the breakfast dishes when he heard his mom coming downstairs. Bo had already left for guide dog class and wouldn't be home until dinner time. "Please go up and finish getting ready, Sycamore," said Charlotte. "I'll clean the sink, and we'll be on our way."

Sycamore hurried to wash his face, brush his teeth, and comb his fur. He was especially careful to wash behind his ears. Today was a day for looking his best. He and Charlotte were going shopping downtown. Shopping for school! Sycamore would be starting kindergarten in exactly one week.

Today he and Charlotte would be shopping for a new collar, a raincoat, and, most important, his first dog license. Sycamore could hardly wait to hear his name tag jingle with the license when he walked. Charlotte had also promised they could eat lunch together at the downtown Burger Barn. That was one of Sycamore's favorite things to do. He loved french fries!

This afternoon, Sycamore had another special appointment. His mom hadn't told him much about it. He only knew he would see Dr. Julie, and she would give him something important that he had to have before starting kindergarten. Sycamore wondered what that might be.

It was a short walk downtown. Sycamore and Charlotte arrived at Randolph's department store at ten o'clock, just as Mr. Randolph was unlocking the door. "Good morning, Charlotte. Hello, Sycamore," he said. "Getting ready for school, I'll bet." Charlotte smiled and Sycamore nodded excitedly.

"I'm sure you have everything we need right here," said Charlotte. Sycamore had fun picking out collars and coats. He tried on six different styles of each. Finally he and Charlotte decided the red collar went best with the gray raincoat. Sycamore's fur was all different colors, so that didn't matter. Charlotte paid Mr. Randolph, and they were on their way.

The next stop was City Hall. "Hello, Charlotte," said Mr. Gibson, as Sycamore and his mom walked into the office. Mr. Gibson worked behind the license desk. "Time to get the pup a tag, I'll bet."

27

"Yes, it is," said Charlotte. She introduced Sycamore to Mr. Gibson and said, "Sycamore starts kindergarten next week."

"Good for you, Sycamore," said Mr. Gibson. "You'll be needing a rabies tag then." Sycamore wondered what rabies was. Then Mr. Gibson asked, "Have you been to see Dr. Julie?"

"Not yet," said Charlotte. "Our appointment is right after lunch."

"That's fine," said Mr. Gibson. "Dr. Julie will call me. Here's your license." Charlotte paid Mr. Gibson, and she and Sycamore went to lunch.

French fries made Sycamore forget all about rabies, though he did wonder how Mr. Gibson knew Dr. Julie. Burger Barn fries were the best!

After lunch, Sycamore and Charlotte walked to Dr. Julie's office. Sycamore had been there once before when he was very little. He could remember the smell. It wasn't a bad smell, really, just different from anything else.

As he waited to see the doctor, Sycamore looked around the room. There were two other puppies with their moms. Over in the corner Sycamore saw a large white bird with a long neck. "Who's that?" whispered Sycamore to his mom.

"I think her name is Cynthia," Charlotte said. "She's a goose, and she lives down the street from us, next to the fire station. Mr. Gibson told me her family is new in town." Sycamore wondered if geese had to have licenses. He looked at Cynthia and thought he saw her smile.

"Sycamore, you're next." It was Dr. Julie. He and Charlotte followed the doctor into another room, and Dr. Julie put Sycamore on a table. She scratched behind his ears and smiled. The table under him was cold, but Sycamore smiled back anyway.

"You're a bright-eyed little pup, Sycamore," said Dr. Julie. "I can tell you eat your carrots." Charlotte smiled. Sycamore didn't like carrots much at all, but he had to eat them anyway. Dr. Julie shined a light into Sycamore's eyes and ears. Then she put a small tube into Sycamore's nose and shined the light again. The tube smelled like the rest of Dr. Julie's office, only stronger.

She patted and poked his belly and scratched his tail. Sycamore liked the scratching better than the poking. Dr. Julie parted his fur and looked very closely at his skin. "No fleas," she said. "Excellent! Charlotte, you have a healthy pup!"

Turning to Sycamore, Dr. Julie said, "Now little one, you're going to feel a little pinch, and it might hurt for a bit." Dr. Julie was right! Before Sycamore could say anything, something very

sharp stuck him just under the shoulder. He yelped! "What was that?" Then he whimpered.

"That," said Dr. Julie, "was a rabies shot."

"What's rabies?" asked Sycamore, trying not to cry. He had quickly learned what a shot was.

"Rabies is a serious disease we don't want you to have to worry about," said Dr. Julie. "I'm sorry about the shot, but it's the only way to be sure you won't get very sick." Gently, she brushed a tear from the corner of Sycamore's eye. Charlotte patted his head.

"You were very brave," said Dr. Julie. "Shots are no fun, but the hurt doesn't last very long, I promise." She reached into a drawer and gave Sycamore one of his favorite puppy biscuits. Dr. Julie told him he could eat it right away. Charlotte nodded. Sycamore tried to smile and then crunched his treat.

It was a quiet walk home. Sycamore was tired. He thought about next week. He wondered if kindergarten would be anything like obedience training or Sunday school. Would he know anyone in his class? He thought about Cynthia, and wondered if she would be starting school too.

When they got home and went inside, Sycamore and Charlotte smelled something very good cooking on the stove. Bo had come home early and supper was almost ready—roast beef and rawhide stew. Sycamore's favorite! And no carrots!

As the three of them sat down to eat, Sycamore asked if he could say grace. He folded his paws. So did Bo and Charlotte. "Dear God," said Sycamore, "thank you for helping us get ready for kindergarten today. Please help us next week too. Bless my mom and dad, and the supper my dad made. And bless Dr. Julie, too. Amen."

NOTES: Most children eagerly anticipate their first day at school, and with adequate preparation this new experience can be a positive one. Preparing the child for this new experience is similar to getting ready to start Sunday school. The more information the child has, the better prepared he or she will be to handle this new situation.

In this story, Sycamore has another experience—going to the doctor. This is often a negative experience for young children. As this story illustrates, with a little preparation and explanation, children can learn that preventative visits to the doctor, while sometimes uncomfortable, are necessary.

As with all other new and different experiences that the child might have, be accepting of his or her feelings. Mixed emotions are normal; everyone has them. Tell your child how you feel when facing a new experience and how you cope with those feelings.

Sycamore and Cynthia —Friends

It was Friday morning, and though it was only the first week, Sycamore decided he was going to like kindergarten. His class did lots of the things Sycamore liked to do already; they listened to stories, drew pictures with paint, and played games. It was especially fun to do all that at school because there were so many more people to play with and learn from.

There were nine boys and eleven girls in Sycamore's class, plus one puppy, of course, and also a very pretty white goose named Cynthia. Sycamore remembered seeing her at Dr. Julie's the day he got his rabies shot.

Cynthia was shy around all the boys and girls, since most of them had never met a goose personally before. But on the second day of school she did smile and say "Hi" to Sycamore when he said "Hi" first. Since then, they had sat next to each other during snack time, and yesterday they played catch at the very end of recess.

Today, Mr. Leland, their teacher, was reviewing the sounds made by the letters of the alphabet. Many of the boys and girls, and Sycamore too, had learned the letters at home before starting school, so this particular lesson was easy.

Sycamore looked across the room to the window where Cynthia was sitting. He noticed that she wasn't paying attention to Mr. Leland. Instead, she was staring outside, looking kind of sad. Sycamore wondered what Cynthia was thinking about.

Just then it happened. Sycamore heard Mr. Leland say, "Cynthia, do you know what sound 'D' makes?" Cynthia jumped and looked to the front of the room, but she didn't say anything. Mr. Leland asked again if Cynthia knew the sound.

Cynthia looked down at the table and said, almost too quietly for Sycamore to hear, "I'm sorry, Mr. Leland, I wasn't paying attention, but I think that letter says 'duh.' "

" 'D' does say 'duh,' " said Mr. Leland. "That's very good. Cynthia, you're learning your sounds. But you'll have to learn to pay attention, too, because we'll soon be making words out of these sounds, and that's much more difficult."

Cynthia was usually a very good goose, and she was not at all used to being scolded. She wiped her eye with her wing as Mr. Leland continued with the letter lesson.

Later that morning, toward the end of snack time, Sycamore went over to Cynthia. She was standing by herself near the window and looking at the terrarium. Not knowing quite what else to say, Sycamore just said, "Hi."

Quietly, and without looking away from the terrarium, Cynthia said, "Hi" back.

Wanting to help, but not knowing exactly how to be helpful, Sycamore said, "Too bad you got yelled at."

Still not looking up, Cynthia said quickly, "I didn't get yelled at. Mr. Leland doesn't yell." And then, her own voice rising almost to a squawk, she continued, "I wish everybody would just leave me alone!"

Sycamore was stunned. He wasn't used to being scolded either, especially by someone he wanted to be friends with. Quietly he said, "I'm sorry." Then he went back to his seat.

All the rest of the day, Sycamore found it hard to pay attention to schoolwork. Something was the matter with Cynthia. He had known that when he saw her staring out the window. He really wanted to be her friend; but now he didn't know what to say to her, and he was beginning to feel alone himself.

When the bell rang for school to be over, Sycamore took his time walking out of the room. He would have to wait for a while at the school gate for his dad to pick him up. On Fridays, Bo's class at guide dog school finished early. Since Sycamore's school was on Bo's way home, Sycamore was going to wait for his dad, and the two of them would walk home together.

As Sycamore walked toward the door, he heard Mr. Leland call Cynthia and ask to talk to her. Sycamore hoped Mr. Leland wasn't going to scold her again. He looked over his shoulder and saw the teacher brush Cynthia's eye with a tissue.

It was a warm afternoon and Sycamore found a tree near the school gate to curl up under to wait for his dad. The grass was cool, and enough sun was shining through the branches to keep Sycamore comfortable. As he closed his eyes, Sycamore heard a quiet voice from behind him call his name. It was Cynthia.

"I'm sorry I yelled at you," she said.

"It's OK," said Sycamore, although now he was really puzzled.

"Whatcha doing?" she asked.

"Sleeping, kind of," Sycamore responded. "I have to wait for my dad to come by, and we're going to walk home together."

At the mention of Sycamore's dad, Cynthia turned her head away. "Does your dad get out of work this early?" she asked.

"My dad doesn't work," Sycamore said. "He lost his job a couple of months ago. Now he goes to school, and he's learning to be a guide dog."

Without turning back to look at Sycamore, Cynthia spoke quietly. "My dad was going to change jobs, too. He's up north now, and he was going to get a transfer here. That's why we moved. But now he's changed his mind."

Sycamore turned to look at Cynthia. "Are you going to move back up north?" he asked.

Tears started to form in Cynthia's eyes. "No," she said. "I'm going to stay here with my mom. My dad's not coming here. They're getting divorced."

Now Sycamore understood why Cynthia looked so sad this morning. He was quiet for a moment; then he reached over and brushed a tear from Cynthia's eye with the back of his paw. Furry paws were good for that. Sycamore remembered how sad he had felt when his dad told him about losing his job. And then he remembered something else. "When I'm extra sad," he said, "sometimes it helps to fold my paws and pray a little."

"My mom prayed with me last night," Cynthia said. "I felt a little better."

"I can pray now, I think," said Sycamore.

"OK," Cynthia said, and she folded her wings.

"Dear God," said Sycamore, "we're sad." Then Sycamore didn't say anything. He didn't know what else to say, so he just said, "Amen."

Cynthia looked at Sycamore. "We're friends, aren't we?"

Sycamore nodded, and then he said, "I think you're nice."

Cynthia nodded. "You are, too." Just then, Cynthia's mom drove up to the curb in front of Sycamore and Cynthia. "I have to go," Cynthia said. "I'll see you Monday."

Sycamore saw Cynthia wave as the car pulled away, and he also thought he saw her smile just a little, too.

NOTES: *Making friends is an important part of growing up for young children. They need to have opportunities to meet and interact with other children in order to develop social skills. While young children* often have casual friendships, they are capable of developing deeper relationships with one another and becoming involved with one another's problems. They sometimes have the ability to offer comfort to another child more effectively than an adult does.

Through their friendships, children can learn about life situations different from or similar to their own. While this can be a good thing, it can also raise questions which will need answering. Sycamore will undoubtedly have questions about divorce as a result of his friendship with Cynthia. The child with whom you are sharing this book might also have questions about friendship or about divorce as a result of reading this story about Sycamore and Cynthia. Listen to the child's questions and answer them honestly.

Children who have experienced divorce in their own families will be able to identify closely with Cynthia. Use this story as an opportunity for them to talk about their feelings.

Trying to Understand About Divorce

It had been a quiet weekend for Sycamore. Yesterday it had rained for most of the afternoon, and Sycamore spent the time cleaning up his room. Both his mom and dad had other work to do over the weekend, so Sycamore was especially careful not to bother them with a lot of questions. However, he did have one very important question to ask his mom when he got the chance.

Sunday supper was over, and Sycamore was coloring in the living room while his dad watched a football game on television. Bo had finished his guide dog school homework that afternoon, and he was resting. At school he was learning to guide people across busy streets, and tomorrow he would be working on a real street for the first time. Charlotte was preparing the next month's work schedule, and she had to give it to the fire chief first thing Monday morning.

Sycamore finished coloring a page in his coloring book and went to ask his mom for a sheet of paper to draw his own picture. When he got back to the living room, he looked around for something to draw. He was about to ask Bo for an idea when he noticed his dad had fallen asleep in the recliner. Deciding not to wake him, Sycamore began to draw a picture of the big dog and the old chair.

Sycamore had the drawing about half finished when his mom came into the room. Quietly Sycamore asked his mom his question. "Is Cynthia's mom nice?"

Somewhat startled, but also fairly sure why Sycamore had asked, Charlotte said, "Yes, I like Audrey very much. She comes over to the firehouse for coffee and we talk."

"Do you talk about Cynthia's dad?" Sycamore wanted to know.

"Sometimes," said Charlotte.

Sycamore had spent much of the weekend thinking about Cynthia and her family, and he was having trouble understanding why nice people got divorced. He had another important question. "If Cynthia's mom is nice, why doesn't Cynthia's dad want to come and live here with her?"

"Sycamore," Charlotte said, "what's happening to Cynthia and her family is very hard to explain. Even Cynthia's mom can't

36

explain all about why she and Cynthia's dad can't live together anymore. They still care about what happens to everyone in the family. Both of them love Cynthia very much, and everyone is sad."

The more Sycamore thought about it, the more confused he got. "If they're so sad, why don't they not get divorced?" he asked.

"I wish it were that simple," said Charlotte. "Sometimes, even though getting divorced is sad, staying together would be even more difficult. In order to live together happily, people have to do more than get along; they have to agree most of the time about how to live as a family. Sometimes, even though people still care about each other, they just can't agree anymore, and it's better for everybody if they make some changes."

By this time Bo was awake and was listening to the conversation. "We've made some changes in our family, too," he said. "Mom and I were able to agree about what to do when I lost my job. But those kinds of changes are never easy. And sometimes things change so much that families split up."

"Is our family going to split up?" Sycamore could feel his nose start to get warm.

Both Charlotte and Bo answered together, "No." Charlotte continued, "The changes that have happened to us have made us closer. But it doesn't always happen like that for everybody. Changes affect different families in different ways, and that's why divorce is so hard to understand."

"If divorce is so hard to understand," Sycamore wondered, "how can I help? Cynthia seems so sad."

"I asked Cynthia's mom the same question," Charlotte answered. "She just asked me to be her friend and to listen to her. That's what I'm trying to do."

"Me, too," Sycamore said. "When I see Cynthia tomorrow I'll try to be extra nice."

"Just be yourself," said Charlotte. "You are a very nice pup. Cynthia needs good friends, and I'm glad she likes you."

The next day, Sycamore and Cynthia ate together during snack time. As they were finishing their milk, Cynthia asked Sycamore, "Will you walk home with me after school? My mom has a meeting downtown, and she can't pick me up. I mostly know my way home, but it's more fun to walk with someone else."

"Sure," said Sycamore. He had walked home by himself two days last week. It was kind of lonely doing that. And since Cynthia lived only two blocks down the street from him, he knew the way home for her, too.

After school was over, Sycamore and Cynthia began the walk home. Cynthia was quiet, so Sycamore asked, "Did you have to stay inside while it was raining Saturday?"

"No," Cynthia said. "I like rain. It wasn't cold, so my mom said I could go out and swim in the puddles. Only on the sidewalk, though."

It was hard for Sycamore to imagine anyone swimming in the rain. He didn't even like the bathtub. But geese were different from puppies, and he supposed Cynthia wouldn't enjoy chewing on a rawhide stick very much, either.

Then Cynthia said, "My dad called me yesterday. He told me he loved me."

"Is he coming to live with you?" Sycamore asked, hopefully.

"No," Cynthia said quietly. "That's what my mom's meeting is about. I guess they'll be divorced in about two weeks." Both the pup and the goose were quiet for a minute. Sycamore didn't know what to say, so he just listened for Cynthia to say more. Cynthia continued, "My dad told me on the phone that he would come and get me next weekend and take me for a visit to where I used to live. He said that someday I would understand." Cynthia sniffed. "I want to understand now."

"Did your mom tell you why your dad isn't moving here?" Sycamore asked.

" No," said Cynthia. "I knew that my mom and dad were sad and that sometimes they argued. My dad was gone a lot with his job. I thought it would be better when he took a new job here." Cynthia wiped her beak with her wing. "I miss my dad. Last night, just before I went to bed, my mom told me that there were problems that go way back to before I was born, and that it's not my fault that they are getting a divorce. Then we both cried.

"I cried some more after my mom kissed me good-night. That's when it's the hardest and when I really feel alone. Sometimes I wonder if I'll always be sad."

"That's when I pray," Sycamore said. "I get sad late at night, too. So that's when I talk to God."

"Where did you learn how to pray?" Cynthia asked.

Sycamore answered, "From Pastor Paul at church and from my teacher, Mrs. Lewis, at Sunday school. We pray at home, too, and that really helped when my dad lost his job."

"Do you think I can learn how to pray?" Cynthia wanted to know.

"Yes," said Sycamore. "You can come with me next Sunday if

you want. I always walk to Sunday school, and I have to go almost past your house to get there.''

Cynthia sounded excited. ''I'll ask my mom,'' she said. ''And maybe she'll talk to your mom. I'd like to meet your friends. I don't have too many friends here yet. Just you.''

Sycamore's nose started to get warm again. He looked up and realized he was in front of his own house. He smiled at Cynthia and she smiled back. ''I'll talk to my mom about Sunday school,'' he said, ''and I'll see you tomorrow.''

''OK,'' Cynthia said. ''Thanks for walking with me.''

Late that night, after his mom had kissed him good-night and turned out the light, Sycamore thought about Cynthia again. He folded his paws. ''Dear God,'' he said, ''help Cynthia when she's sad. Help us try to understand. Amen.''

NOTES: Divorce is difficult for children to understand. They often blame themselves for the troubles in the family. The tensions in the household affect everyone, and often parents are so tied up in their own emotions that they don't take the time to explain to the children what is happening. Finding a quiet time to sit together and talk about this difficult issue is very important. Praying about the problem and the feelings we have about it will also offer comfort.

Children who are not experiencing divorce in their own families will also have questions and concerns about divorce. Like Sycamore, the children might wonder whether or not their parents will divorce one another as a result of conflicts or changes. Be alert to such concerns, and try to allay their fears as they surface.

Bo, the Guide Dog

Sycamore walked into the kitchen just as his dad was finishing a phone conversation. "Thanks, Pastor Paul," Bo said. "If this works out, it would certainly answer a lot of questions I've been asking myself for the last three months . . . We'll all see you tomorrow night . . . Thanks again . . . Good-bye."

"You always say puppies are the only ones who have lots of questions," said Sycamore, picking up his coloring book from the counter.

"That's true for a little puppy I know whose name is Sycamore," said Bo. "You ask questions all day long."

"I do?" asked Sycamore. "How come you always say that? How else do you expect me to learn anything? What were you and Pastor Paul talking about anyway?"

Rolling his eyes, Bo said, "Is it all right with you if I just answer your last question?"

"Yes," said Sycamore, because Pastor Paul's phone call was what he was most curious about.

"Pastor Paul called with what might be very good news," Bo said. "He told me he had talked to Mr. Albert, the man who teaches my guide dog class, about someone in our congregation who might need to hire a guide dog." Sycamore could think of a guide dog who needed a job. Bo would graduate from school next week. Bo continued, "Pastor Paul told Mr. Albert about Mrs. Langdon."

Sycamore knew who Mrs. Langdon was. She was a nice lady with gray hair who walked slowly and always sat three rows behind him in church. On Sunday mornings she would reach out and scratch Sycamore behind the ears on her way back from receiving Communion. That always made him smile.

"About three months ago," Bo said, "Mrs. Langdon had surgery on her eyes. The doctor who did the operation hoped it might keep her from going blind, but it didn't work very well. Mrs. Langdon can hardly see at all anymore." Now that Sycamore thought about it, Mrs. Langdon hadn't reached out to scratch him lately. She probably couldn't even see him! Sycamore felt sad.

Bo went on, "Tomorrow night Pastor Paul is going to visit Mrs. Langdon. He has invited you, your mother, Mr. Albert, and me to go with him. It just might be that Mrs. Langdon will want me to be her guide dog!"

Suddenly Sycamore felt very excited. For the last three months he had tried not to think much about it, but he did wonder what his dad would do when guide dog classes were over. He had heard his mom and dad talking together, wondering if Bo would have a chance to get a new job once he had learned to be a guide dog. Tomorrow night maybe they would all know for sure.

The next day all Sycamore could think about was meeting Mrs. Langdon. In his excitement, he forgot to take his milk money to school. He had to borrow a quarter from Cynthia to have milk with his puppy biscuit lunch. He told her about going to meet Mrs. Langdon, and Cynthia got nervous and excited, too.

That night, after supper, the whole family hurried to get cleaned up. Bo and Charlotte brushed each other's fur, and Sycamore put on his red collar. They were all sitting in the living room when Mr. Albert came to pick them up. Bo introduced him to Charlotte and Sycamore, and the four of them climbed into Mr. Albert's van.

"Now don't be nervous, Bo," said Mr. Albert. "I told Pastor Paul you were one of the best guide dogs I ever trained. It sounds to me like Mrs. Langdon might be just the person for you to work with." Sycamore hoped Mr. Albert was right.

As they slowed to a stop in front of Mrs. Langdon's house, Sycamore could see Pastor Paul's car in the driveway. As Sycamore's family and Mr. Albert came up the walk, Pastor Paul opened the door. "Welcome!" he said. "Mrs. Langdon asked me to show you in."

When everyone was inside, Mrs. Langdon got up from her chair and asked to meet Mr. Albert. Mr. Albert took her by the hand and introduced himself. Then he said, "Mrs. Langdon, I'm very happy to meet you, and I'm pleased to introduce Bo to you. I've been working with him for the last three months, and he's the smartest, most gentle dog in the class."

"I'm pleased to meet you too, sir," said Mrs. Langdon. "The work you do training guide dogs is just wonderful." Mr. Albert smiled. "And Bo," she continued, "I was so happy when Pastor Paul told me you were graduating from Mr. Albert's class. I've seen you and your family in church. That is, I saw you when I could see. Your little pup is such a dear." Sycamore felt his nose start to get warm. He smiled.

42

"Now, Mrs. Langdon," said Mr. Albert, "we train our dogs to guide you anywhere you want to go. They are also able to help you around the house."

"I don't know about that," said Mrs. Langdon. "I know my way around the house pretty well. I've lived here over fifty years! Besides, I'm not at all sure I want lots of dog hair on my good furniture and oriental rug." Bo jumped a little and Sycamore blushed again.

"Nothing personal," said Mrs. Langdon, softening. "I really only need someone to help me get to the market, the department store, and, of course, to church. Those are about the only places I ever go by myself, and I surely want to be able to continue going on my own. Besides, Bo needn't stay here all day. He should spend time with his family." Bo relaxed. Mrs. Langdon continued, "I'm not one to sit around or ask other people to cart me all over the place. I love to walk. It's only three blocks uptown and two blocks to church. I'll pay full-time wages to any guide dog who helps me live just the way I've always lived."

"Bo could certainly help you do that and more, Mrs. Langdon," said Mr. Albert. "I've taught him to ride in a taxi, use the hospital elevator, watch for traffic lights, and wait for the bus. He could also go with you to restaurants, the library, anywhere at all!"

"I haven't been to the library in months," said Mrs. Langdon. "I did love to go there, but since I can't see to read, there's not much sense in making the trip anymore."

"Mrs. Langdon," said Mr. Albert, "the library has a new section with many stories on cassettes and many books in Braille, too."

"As you talk about what Bo and I could do," said Mrs. Langdon, "it sounds too good to be true."

"Maybe the best thing for you to do," said Mr. Albert, "is to go with Bo and me for a walk. He could take you to church and back, and I'll teach you to use Bo's special collar and harness." Everyone agreed that was a fine idea.

Since there was a slipcover on the back of Mrs. Langdon's couch, Sycamore sat there, looking out the front window all the while his dad was gone. After what seemed like forever, he saw them coming up the walk. As Charlotte went out to meet them, Sycamore jumped from the couch into Pastor Paul's lap. When Mrs. Langdon opened the door, Sycamore heard her say, "Bo, you were wonderful!"

Mr. Albert patted Bo and scratched his ears. They all came inside and sat down again in Mrs. Langdon's living room. Mrs.

Langdon nodded to Mr. Albert and said, "Bo and I are going to get along fine. As far as I'm concerned, the sooner he starts, the better!"

"I kind of thought this arrangement might work," said Mr. Albert. "Bo graduates next week, and he can begin working as soon after that as you and he can work out the details."

Pastor Paul smiled and scratched Sycamore's ears. "I've known Mrs. Langdon for a long time," he said. "She'll be a pleasure to work with."

"Pastor Paul," said Mrs. Langdon, "now that all this is settled, will you say a prayer for us?"

"I'd like that," he said. They all bowed their heads and Sycamore folded his paws. "Dear Lord," said Pastor Paul, "thank you for guide dogs and for the people who train them. Bless Mr. Albert and everyone he works with. Help Bo and Mrs. Langdon as they get to know each other and work together. Keep us all in your grace. Amen."

Charlotte and Sycamore looked at Bo. All three of them winked.

NOTES: Most young children have had no experience with guide dogs or what they can do. This story provides an excellent opportunity for you to introduce this topic to your child.

People who are blind can be very independent in their daily lives with the aid of a guide dog. These carefully trained dogs permit people who are blind to go places and do things that would be impossible on their own. Of course, guide dogs in real life live with the people they are trained to work with, but the story does provide basic information about the work that such dogs do. This story and the books suggested in the bibliography can help your child become more sensitive to the world in which people who are blind live and the independence that is available to them.

Sycamore and Cynthia Meet a Bully

Friday afternoons were special for Sycamore. Every other day of the week his mom finished working at the firehouse in time to be home when Sycamore arrived from school. On Fridays, however, the night shift fire dog didn't come in until seven o'clock, so Charlotte stayed late.

Friday was also Mrs. Langdon's day to get her hair done, and Bo worked with her all day. Mrs. Langdon always enjoyed going out once she had her hair fixed, so each Friday she and Bo had supper at a restaurant after they left the beauty shop.

Sycamore couldn't cook his own supper, and, since no one else was there to do it for him, other arrangements had to be made. It was those other arrangements that made Friday afternoons special.

Instead of walking to his house after school, Sycamore went to the firehouse and stayed to have supper with his mom and the fire fighters. That meant he could walk two blocks farther with Cynthia.

Cynthia lived next door to the firehouse, and the two of them enjoyed walking home from kindergarten together. They were good friends, and they used the time walking home from school to talk. Sometimes they talked about Sycamore's dad's new job. Sometimes they talked about church. On the weekends that Cynthia wasn't visiting her dad, she went to Sunday school with Sycamore, and Audrey went to church with Bo and Charlotte.

Sometimes Sycamore and Cynthia talked about Cynthia's parents' divorce. That was still very sad, but Mrs. Lewis, Pastor Paul, and Mr. Leland were helping Sycamore, Cynthia, and their families try to understand.

Sycamore and Cynthia also talked about anything else that seemed important at the time. Today, as they walked past Sycamore's house on their way to Cynthia's, they talked about their favorite subject in school—art class. That week Sycamore and Cynthia had learned to paint, but not with a brush. Their teacher called it finger painting, even though for a puppy and a goose it was more

like paw and claw painting. Sycamore and Cynthia each had a freshly painted drawing ready to be hung on their refrigerators.

They were walking past a large hedge when, out of the corner of his eye, Sycamore thought he saw something move. What he saw was two boys who jumped out from behind the hedge and blocked their path. "It's fur-face and feather-brain!" said one of the boys, nastily.

The other, who was wearing a dirty cowboy hat, said, "I could use a goose feather for my new hat. Let's get one!"

Cynthia squawked and began to run. The boy with the hat picked up a stick, and they both began to chase her.

Sycamore didn't move. At first he was frightened. Then he realized that these were the same two bullies who, when he was very little, had chased him and pulled his tail. The boys were brothers, and they lived in the house with the hedge. No one liked them very much.

Sycamore saw the boys chase Cynthia around the back of the house next door. He ran around that house from the other direction. Sycamore passed Cynthia and ran toward the two boys as fast as he could. Before they even knew he was there, Sycamore jumped and grabbed the stick from the boy with the hat.

Suddenly everyone stopped—everyone but Cynthia, that is. Sycamore saw her keep running until she was hidden behind a tree. The boys and Sycamore eyed each other. The boy with the hat took a step in Sycamore's direction. Sycamore, still with the stick in his mouth, bared his teeth and growled.

"Fur-face thinks he's tough," said the boy with the hat. As he said that, his partner took a step toward Sycamore. Sycamore growled gain and broke the stick with his teeth. He dropped one jagged half on the grass in front of him. The boy with the hat saw Sycamore's teeth and said, "Uh, maybe we've had enough fun with these, uh, two ANIMALS! Let's go home. I just thought of somethin' I gotta do."

"I'll bet," thought Sycamore. "They'll probably think of someone else to pick on—someone without teeth!"

As the boys sauntered away, Sycamore turned the other way and went to the tree that hid Cynthia. Dropping the half of the stick he still had in his mouth, he said, quietly, "They're gone."

Cynthia slowly came out from behind the tree. "They're so mean," she said. "They've chased me before when I was alone. Thank you."

"They're not so tough," said Sycamore, feeling his nose start to

48

get warm. "They just have big mouths. Without a stick, they can't scare anyone, at least not for long. Let's go find your mom."

Actually, Sycamore was puzzled. He hadn't ever done anything to either of the boys. As far as he could tell, they teased him and Cynthia because of their fur and feathers. Sycamore thought Cynthia's feathers were pretty. And his fur, even though it was funny colored, was very soft and kept him warm.

Cynthia's house was four doors away. When they reached the front door, they found a note from Audrey, Cynthia's mom. It said, "Cynthia, Sycamore, come to the firehouse. Love, Mom."

Still a little nervous from being chased, Sycamore and Cynthia went next door. They found Audrey and Charlotte having coffee in the living room of the firehouse. The pup and the goose ran to their moms. Though she had been trying not to cry all the way home, Cynthia began to sniffle. Puzzled, Audrey asked, "What's the matter?"

Charlotte looked at Sycamore. Quietly he and Cynthia told Charlotte and Audrey all about the boys, the stick, fur-face and feather-brain, and about how the boys went away when Sycamore growled and broke the stick.

"Lucky for them you're just a pup," said Charlotte. "I wish we never had to act mean or get mad. But fur-face and feather-brain! I can't believe someone would chase you with sticks just because you're different." She scratched Sycamore's ears.

Audrey was holding Cynthia on her lap. Cynthia wiped her beak on her mom's coffee napkin. Then Charlotte went into the kitchen and brought Sycamore and Cynthia two cookies each and some lemonade. As they munched their treats, the two began to relax. "I'm OK now," said Cynthia. "Sycamore's my friend." Sycamore smiled.

The four of them began to talk about school and about art class. It was then that Sycamore and Cynthia remembered their paintings. Both had dropped them when the boys jumped from behind the hedge. "Perhaps we'll find them on the way home," said Charlotte. "But, if not, you can paint another one next week, can't you?"

Before Cynthia and Sycamore could answer, they were startled by a loud noise. It was a bell, followed by a buzz, and then the bell rang again. Immediately Charlotte jumped up and looked at the loudspeaker on the wall. A voice from the speaker said, "Ladder Company 7. Engine Company 4. Rescue 9. Active alarm, Shady Lane Apartments, 12th and Oak."

Quickly Charlotte said, "An active alarm at an apartment building means someone pulled the fire box in a hallway. We're Engine 4 and we'll have to hurry." A flurry of activity had begun as the fire fighters rushed to put on their helmets, coats, and boots. As she trotted toward the truck, Charlotte called over her shoulder. "Sycamore, go home and wait for your father. He'll heat up some leftovers for your supper. I may be late."

Audrey called to Charlotte, "I'll take Sycamore home and feed him. Don't worry. And be careful!"

One of the fire fighters handed Charlotte her helmet as she jumped on the truck. Turning to Audrey, Cynthia, and Sycamore, she smiled and waved as the big truck rolled out the door.

Sycamore walked next door with Cynthia and her mom. As they went inside, he could still hear the siren from his mom's truck in the distance. Quickly folding his paws, he said, quietly, "Dear God, watch over my mom. Amen."

NOTES: *When children come in contact with other children, the issue of bullies is almost inevitable. Children need to be taught techniques for coping with bullying behavior. These will vary depending on the age and temperament of the child involved. Sycamore stood up to the bullies in this story, and they backed off. Sometimes that approach works. Sometimes the best thing for a child to do is to run away to an adult who can intervene. Still other children seem to have an innate skill for dealing with bullies.*

Help your child realize that he or she need not be bullied, and explore a variety of ways that such behavior can be dealt with. One way to do this would be for you and the child to role-play situations. You could take on the role of a bully, and the child can pretend to respond to the bully's behavior. After a while you might reverse roles.

Charlotte's Fire

Bo heard Mrs. Langdon call after him as he climbed into the police car. "I'll call Pastor Paul," she said.

On their way to the hospital, Bo asked the police officer if she knew anything about the fire. She didn't know any more than Bo did, and he had talked to the fire chief. The chief had called Bo at Mrs. Langdon's and then sent the police car to pick him up. All anyone knew for sure was that Charlotte was hurt.

The chief told Bo how it happened. He had sent Charlotte and Fireman Pete into the burning apartment building to find a child who was lost inside. Actually, Charlotte had volunteered to go since she could search with her sharp nose and ears as well as her eyes.

Most of the flames had been put out by the time the fire fighters began the search, though the fire had done a lot of damage to the old two-story building. Charlotte and Fireman Pete had searched the ground floor and found nothing, so they went upstairs. It wasn't long before Charlotte found the three-year-old boy huddled under a blanket in a back bedroom. She had heard him cry through the closed door and barked to Fireman Pete, who came and picked up the child.

As the three of them hurried toward the stairs, the floor began to give way beneath them. Fireman Pete, carrying the little boy, reached the stairs ahead of the cave-in. Charlotte did not, and she fell through to the floor below.

Moving quickly, Fireman Pete carried the child outside and ran back to help Charlotte. He found her crawling out from under a pile of debris, struggling for the door. Carefully, but without delay, Fireman Pete carried Charlotte out of the building and helped load her into a waiting ambulance. As they covered her with a blanket, Charlotte said, "Tell Bo it's just my leg." Then she and the little boy were whisked to the hospital.

When the chief called Bo, he gave him Charlotte's message. That still didn't stop Bo from worrying. He bounded out of the police car toward the hospital's emergency room entrance just as the vehicle came to a stop. The fire chief was there already, waiting for him at the door. The two of them hurried back into the waiting room.

"Dr. Julie was here at the hospital with another patient," said the chief. "She came right down when they brought Charlotte in. I don't know for sure how badly Charlotte is hurt, but I did hear her answering Dr. Julie's questions about what happened. She's a mighty brave fire dog."

Bo was relieved to hear Charlotte was alert and talking to the doctor. Knowing that made the wait a little less anxious.

Waiting was all there was to do, and it wasn't long before Pastor Paul joined them. "Have you heard anything?" he asked. Bo and the chief told Pastor Paul all they knew, and the three of them continued to wait.

"I've worried about something like this for a long time," Bo said. "Only last week Sycamore asked me if . . . SYCAMORE!" Bo jumped up. "He must be home alone! It's nearly seven o'clock and I was supposed to be home half an hour ago."

"I think I can help," said Pastor Paul. "It's usually a long wait here. If you'd like, I'll go now and bring Sycamore to the hospital. He knows me pretty well, and I think I can tell him about Charlotte gently."

"That would help a lot," said Bo. "I'm sure we'll still be waiting when you get back." He slumped into his chair.

Sycamore had walked home from Cynthia's house and arrived about the time he expected his dad to be home from Mrs. Langdon's. He was surprised to find the house empty. Not knowing quite what else to do with himself, Sycamore got out his crayons and paper and began to draw. Nothing like this had ever happened before.

He was nervously working on a picture of his mom and a fire truck when he heard a car in front of the house. He saw Pastor Paul come up the front walk and was more puzzled than ever. He was quite a bit more nervous, too. Before Pastor Paul could ring the doorbell, Sycamore reached up and opened the door. "No one's home but me!" he exclaimed.

"I know," said Pastor Paul, as Sycamore motioned him inside. "I came here to talk with you about that." Sycamore was suddenly very confused. He sat down on the floor with his crayons.

Gently, Pastor Paul said, "Sycamore, your dad is at the hospital. He's there with your mom. She was hurt this afternoon at the fire." Sycamore's mouth fell open, and his eyes began to fill. Pastor Paul continued, "I just now came from the hospital. I haven't seen your mom yet, but Dr. Julie is with her. Your mom is telling her about how she got hurt."

"Do you know what happened?" asked Sycamore, shakily.

"I'm not completely sure," said Pastor Paul. "I do know she was inside the burning apartment building searching for a little boy. The fire chief seemed to think she hurt her leg in a fall. One of the fire fighters rescued the little boy after your mom found him, and he carried your mom out of the building, too, after she fell."

"Can I see her?" asked Sycamore.

"I came to take you to the hospital," Pastor Paul said. "We may not be able to see her for a while, but you can wait with your dad and me."

It was a quiet ride to the hospital. Pastor Paul stroked Sycamore's fur and gave him a handkerchief to wipe his eyes. When they arrived, Pastor Paul carried the little pup into the emergency room and took him to Bo.

"Mom's hurt!" cried Sycamore, when he saw his dad.

"I know," said Bo, as Pastor Paul sat Sycamore next to his dad. Scratching his son behind the ears, Bo continued. "I'm glad you're here. A minute ago the nurse said that Dr. Julie will be out soon to tell us exactly how mom is."

Just then, the nurse appeared from behind the door and said, "Bo, Dr. Julie is ready to talk to you. You folks can come to a room here in the back."

Bo, Sycamore, Pastor Paul, and the fire chief hurried to where the nurse directed them. Dr. Julie smiled as she met them at the door of the room. Motioning them to be seated, she said, "Charlotte is going to be OK. She has a couple of cuts and bruises, but we've fixed them up already. The X rays we took showed us that her right hind leg is broken. She took quite a fall, and her leg was giving her a lot of pain. I can fix it, but I will have to do a little surgery to set it properly. The nurses are getting her ready now, and I'll take care of it right away." Thinking of his mom in pain started Sycamore crying again, softly. Bo held his paw.

Dr. Julie drew them a picture of what she was going to do and explained how to set a broken leg. Nodding to Bo and Sycamore, she said, "She'll be fine. I'll put a cast on her leg, and I think she'll heal up real well. She's a strong dog, and brave, too."

Sycamore relaxed a bit as Dr. Julie stood to leave. "Can I see her?" he asked.

"I'm afraid not just now," said Dr. Julie. The shot I gave her to relieve the pain also makes her sleepy, and it prepares her for surgery. She's nearly asleep already. But you can see her right after I'm finished. It won't be long, I promise."

Sycamore was thinking about Dr. Julie giving his mom a shot when Pastor Paul spoke. "Before you go," he said to Dr. Julie, "I'd

54

like to pray about the operation."

"A good idea," said Dr. Julie, and everyone nodded in agreement. Sycamore folded his paws.

"Dear Lord," said Pastor Paul, "you promised always to be with us. Help us know you are with us now. Bless Charlotte, and keep her safe through surgery. Guide Dr. Julie's hands with yours, and bless us all with courage and hope. Amen."

"Thank you," said Dr. Julie. As she turned to leave, she looked at Sycamore and winked.

The nurse directed them to another waiting room at the end of the hall. Wait they did. The fire chief watched the news on the corner television. Bo went down the hall for a drink four times, and paced the floor in between trips. Occasionally, Pastor Paul went with him. Sycamore sat on the window sill, looking out over the parking lot.

After what seemed like hours, but was really only forty-five minutes, Dr. Julie came into the room. She had a surgeon's mask in her hand, and she was smiling.

"It all went fine," she said. "Charlotte's just waking up. It wasn't a bad break, as broken legs go, and I'm sure it will heal nicely." She patted Bo and Sycamore. "You can see her in a few minutes, and I'll tell the nurse to come and get you when Charlotte is ready." Everyone nodded and smiled.

"Pastor Paul," asked Sycamore, "would you pray again and tell God thanks?"

"Let's all do that," said Pastor Paul. "Sycamore, fold your paws. Dear Lord, thank you for the gifts of medicine and surgery. Thank you for being with us, and with Dr. Julie and Charlotte. Give Charlotte courage, and the strength she needs to recover. Amen."

"Dr. Julie," said Sycamore, "Thank you too!" Just then, the nurse came into the room and Sycamore skipped down the hall to see his mom.

NOTES: *Hospitalization is a very frightening experience for children. It is not only a change in their routine, but the strange and sometimes painful procedures are also difficult to deal with. In some situations, such as when the hospitalization is planned for elective procedures, the child can be prepared ahead of time. But usually hospitalization is not planned, making it an even more upsetting situation.*

When a parent is ill, injured, or hospitalized, the child will also need much support to cope with the changes and stresses within the family. Be honest as you respond to questions. Offer support as needed, and let the child know that it is perfectly all right to express his or her feelings. Praying together can be a wonderful source of comfort as you and the child face this difficult situation.

Being the Best That We Can Be

As he walked through the family room, Sycamore stopped to look at his mom's new certificate, which was hanging on the wall. "Citation of Merit," it said. A month ago, the mayor had come to Charlotte's hospital room and presented her with the award. "For Outstanding Dedication and Bravery"—that's what the certificate said. When he gave it to her, the mayor told Charlotte that she was an example of "the best that a fire dog can be."

Charlotte was still recovering from having fallen through the floor of the burning apartment building. Just yesterday, Dr. Julie had put a new cast on Charlotte's broken leg. Now she could walk without crutches.

Sycamore walked into the kitchen and climbed up on a stool. Charlotte was making bread, and Sycamore enjoyed watching her knead the dough on the counter. It took a long time to get it just right for baking. While she worked, Charlotte and Sycamore had a chance to talk. "Do I have good ears?" Sycamore asked.

"If you mean, are your ears very sensitive, yes," answered Charlotte.

"Then I could use my ears to find stuff I couldn't see, right?"

"Yes," Charlotte answered again, "if what you were looking for made noise. Why do you ask?"

"I was just wondering," said Sycamore.

Charlotte knew that Sycamore never just wondered. She could tell when he had something on his mind. Casually, she asked, "What were you wondering about?"

Sycamore answered quickly, "Do you think I could've heard that little boy in the apartment building like you did?"

Charlotte turned and looked at her pup. "Maybe so," she said. "What made you think of that?"

Sycamore spoke quietly. "I was thinking, if I'd been up there instead of you, I could've found him and not fallen through the floor, 'cause I'm just little." He looked at his mom's new cast.

"I'm not all that big," said Charlotte, smiling to herself. She knew very well that she would be answering more questions from Sycamore before the afternoon was over. He had not said much about the fire, but Charlotte noticed that he spent a lot of time looking at her certificate and playing with his fire trucks. He had also insisted that Cynthia's painting of Charlotte and her cast be hung on the refrigerator next to his own drawing of the firehouse.

Charlotte didn't have long to wait for his next question. "Are you the best fire dog in the whole world?"

Charlotte looked at Sycamore and winked. "I don't know," she said. "But I'll bet I'm the only one with a pup who's ready to take over the job when his mom's out of commission for a while."

"Are you going back to work?"

Charlotte stopped kneading. She had not expected that question so soon. Actually, it was the very same question she had been asking herself for most of the last month. To answer Sycamore, and to give herself time to think, Charlotte said, "Dr. Julie told me I couldn't go back for six weeks anyway, and then only part-time. So I'll have to wait and see."

"Only the best fire dogs have to go into burning buildings, don't they?"

"Sometimes that's a part of every fire dog's job," Charlotte said. "Fortunately, it doesn't happen very often."

"But it happened to you, didn't it?"

"Yes, it did."

"Were you scared?"

"Yes."

Sycamore sat quietly, looking at his feet. "You can't be the best fire dog in the whole world if you don't go back to the firehouse, can you?"

Charlotte smiled. She had begun to understand what Sycamore was really asking with all his questions. He was proud of his mom, but he was scared too. And he needed to be reminded of something very important.

"Sycamore," Charlotte said, "I don't know if I'm the best fire dog in the whole world. But that isn't what matters most to me. I'm happy when the mayor and the fire chief say nice things about my work. But I'm also happy making bread and talking to you." Sycamore looked up. Charlotte continued, "I want to be the best that I can be. Always. At the firehouse, and here at home. I want that for you too."

She reached out and scratched Sycamore's ears. "As you grow up, one thing I hope you learn is that all of us are the best that we can be when we love each other. And when we care about what happens to those we love. You're my best pup, and I love you."

Sycamore hugged his mom. "I love you, too," he said.

They finished making bread together; then Sycamore went outside to play. He decided to take a walk to the end of the block and back. As he was walking, he thought of something Mrs. Lewis had said at Sunday school. She told the class, "When you know that God loves you, it's easy to love each other."

Sycamore decided his mom knew that God loved her. Sycamore loved her too. And he knew God loved them both.

Later that night, after he and his mom and dad had prayed together and gone to bed, Sycamore folded his paws again. "Dear God," he prayed, "thank you for loving me and my mom and dad. Keep us safe together, and help us be the best that we can be. Amen."

NOTES: As children grow up it is important that they be reminded often of the message of this story. As they are learning new skills and perfecting old ones, there are still so many things that they can't do "until they grow up" or "until they are bigger." It is important to their self concepts that they be reminded of the things that they do well. One child might be the best jumper, while another might have the biggest smile. They can be told that while they might not yet be able to ride a two-wheeler, they are the best tricycle riders on the block. Children should be encouraged to take pride in all of their skills and always try to be the best that they can be.

BIBLIOGRAPHY

Starting School

Cohen, Miriam. *Will I Have a Friend?* New York: Macmillan, 1967.
It is Jim's first day in kindergarten, and he worries that he will not have a friend.

Quackenbush, Robert. *First Grade Jitters.* New York: J. B. Lippincott, 1982.
Piet is worried, cranky, and in fact just not his usual self. He's about to enter first grade and doesn't know what to expect.

Stanek, Muriel. *Starting School.* Niles, Ill.: Albert Whitman & Co., 1981.
A little boy narrates in considerable detail his preparation for school and his first-day experiences. His attitude is positive and practical. The book will be helpful for preschoolers getting ready to start kindergarten.

Forgiveness

Hazen, Barbara Shook. *Even If I Did Something Awful?* New York: Atheneum, 1981.
A child is reassured of her mother's love in spite of a series of made-up catastrophes. The true test occurs when something awful does happen, and the love endures.

Silverstein, Shel. *The Giving Tree.* New York: Harper & Row, 1964.
In spite of the fact that a boy took so much from the tree—its apples, its branches, and even its trunk—the tree shows forgiveness by suggesting that the boy sit on its stump to relax.

Wildsmith, Brian. *The Owl and the Woodpecker.* Salem, N. H. Merrimack Publishers Circle, 1984.
A feud develops when Owl's sleep is disturbed by Woodpecker's pecking all day. When Owl's tree falls during a storm, however, Woodpecker shows forgiveness to Owl by rescuing Owl and helping him find another place to live.

Zolotow, Charlotte. *The Hating Book.* New York: Harper & Row, 1969.
This book describes a situation in which, through a misunderstanding, two friends don't speak to each other for a week. Forgiveness enters the story when one girl approaches the other and they become friends again.

Unemployment

Delton, Judy. *My Mother Lost Her Job Today.* Niles, Ill.: Albert Whitman & Co., 1980.
Young children will easily understand the plight of the little girl in this story who is frightened by the signs of distress in her newly unemployed mother. They will be able to identify with the need to be reassured that life will eventually return to normal.

Hazen, Barbara Shook. *Tight Times.* New York: Viking-Penguin, 1979.
The everyday meaning of economic hard times, parental love, and the company of pets is made clear in this book. The little boy who tells the story perceives his

parents as harried and distressed, and his father explains "tight times" in understandable terms.

Job Retraining

Cleary, Beverly Bunn. *Ramona Quimby, Age Eight*. West Caldwell, N. J.: William Morrow & Co., 1981.
In this story the Quimby family must cope with the changes that come when Mr. Quimby returns to school. Old and new fans of Ramona Quimby will be thoroughly pleased with this book.

Working Mother

Alda, Arlene. *Sonya's Mommy Works*. New York: Simon & Schuster, 1982.
Life is complicated for little Sonya when her mother begins to work away from home. However, with the loving support of both parents, she manages to accept the things she cannot change and live a normal, happy life. Realistic photographs add interest to this honest look at family feelings and adjustments.

Cleary, Beverly Bunn. *Ramona and Her Mother*. West Caldwell, N. J.: William Morrow & Co., 1979.
This funny and touching story shows the struggles of a little girl to cope with changes in her family's life-style resulting from economic bad times. Ramona comes to realize that these changes, while upsetting, do not affect her parents' love for her.

Power, Barbara. *I Wish Laura's Mommy Was My Mommy*. New York: Harper & Row, 1979.
Jennifer comes to appreciate her own home and mother when the "perfect" mother of a friend becomes Jennifer's baby-sitter rather than hostess. This amusing story allows children to compare two life-styles and to evaluate the old adage "The grass is always greener."

Schick, Eleanor. *Home Alone*. New York: Dial Books, 1980.
In this first-person account, a little boy comes home to an empty house for the first time and acts responsibly and is self-reliant. This story is well suited for use by parents and children together as they prepare for a similar new experience.

Smith, Lucia B. *My Mom Got a Job*. New York: Holt, Rinehart & Winston, 1979.
A young girl tells what she likes and what she doesn't like about her life when her mother gets a job. Readers will respond to the cheerful and resourceful manner in which the main character adapts to her changed home life.

Friendships

Brown, Myra Berry. *Best Friends*. Childrens Press, 1967.
This illustrated poem gives many brief examples of the special relationship between two children who are best friends. It clearly shows that this relationship can endure in spite of occasional arguments.

Heine, Helme. *Friends*. New York: Atheneum, 1982.
"Good friends always stick together." That's what Charlie Rooster, Johnny Mouse, and fat Percy, the pig, always said. And that was what they did all day long. This is a joyful book, an exhilarating celebration of friendship.

Divorce

Berger, Terry. *A Friend Can Help*. Milwaukee: Raintree Publishers, 1975.
A young girl narrates her feelings about her parents' divorce to her best friend. The book stresses the importance of having someone to talk to.

Blue, Rose. *A Month of Sundays*. New York: Franklin Watts, 1972.
In this story, a boy deals with the problems of a divorce: seeing his father only on Sundays; moving to the city; his mother's taking a job.

Goff, Beth. *Where Is Daddy?* Boston: Beacon Press, 1969.
An honest, realistic discussion of divorce, this book was written by a psychiatric social worker.

Grollman, Earl. *Talking About Divorce and Separation: A Dialogue Between Parent and Child*. Boston: Beacon Press, 1975.
This book is in two parts (one part for parents to read to the child and one part addressed to the parents) and explains how the child probably interprets the separation announcement. The author deals with the child's feelings of guilt, anger, and confusion.

Lexau, Joan M. *Emily and the Klunky Baby and the Next-Door Dog*. New York: Dial Books, 1972.
Since her parents' divorce, Emily has felt that mother is too busy and doesn't want Emily and her baby brother anymore. The feeling of rejection depicted in this story is often experienced by a child whose parents are divorced.

Newfield, Marcia. *A Book for Jodan*. New York: Atheneum, 1975.
A sensitive story about a nine-year-old girl's fears about being abandoned after her parents' divorce, this book depicts a tender relationship between father and daughter.

Paris, Lena. *Mom Is Single*. Chicago: Childrens Press, 1980.
A boy describes the painful changes that his parents' divorce has brought to their family. Simply told and vividly illustrated with photographs, this story may promote understanding of family upheavals as the boy comes to realize that, despite all the changes, his parents continue to love him.

Schuchman, Joan. *Two Places to Sleep*. Minneapolis: Carolrhoda Books, 1979.
Despite patient, supportive, reassuring parents, a young boy needs time and abundant love to accept the breakup of his family. David's insights—that divorces happen but that parents don't "get divorced from their children" and that he can get used to his new life—have wide application and should provoke useful discussion between parents and children.

Stein, Sara Bonnett. On Divorce (An Open Family Book for Parents and Children Together). New York: Walker & Co., 1984.
A little girl, hearing that her friends' parents are divorcing, fears that her father will leave her. When her parents argue, Becky is sure they will divorce too. Reassured that even people who love each other can disagree, Becky's fears are alleviated. A guide for parents, explaining how the text may be used in relation to the child's feelings, is included on each page, along with the text for the child.

Guide Dog—Blindness

Montgomery, Elizabeth Rider. *"Seeing" in the Dark*. Easton, Md.: Garrard Publishing Co., 1979.
A young blind girl, mainstreamed into a regular classroom, has some trouble making friends at first. But soon her plucky acceptance of her disability wins over her classmates, and she is already a successful class member when she leads the others out of their burning school to safety. The emphasis is on the child's compensation for her blindness: the keenness of her other senses, her musical ability, and her refusal to pity herself or accept pity from others.

Reuter, Margaret. *My Mother Is Blind*. Chicago: Childrens Press, 1979.
A boy describes his mother's and family's adjustment to her blindness. The emphasis is on the mother's strengths and growing independence. Illustrations of a Braille book and of writing in Braille with a stylus are of special interest. The text can easily be understood by young children.

Wolf, Bernard. *Connie's New Eyes*. New York: J. B. Lippincott, 1976.
Through his sensitive photographs and text, Bernard Wolf shows how a guide dog puppy is raised and trained to work with its master. The book then follows the events of Connie David, who has been blind since birth, as she begins her life as a teacher. This is a long book and goes into great detail, but the photographs and parts of the text could be used with even young children.

Bullies

Alexander, Martha G. *Move Over Twerp*. New York: Dial Books, 1981.
A little boy defuses a bully by using both resourcefulness and humor. Although the solution to the child's problem may be oversimplified, it does demonstrate that children can encounter superior force with ingenuity. Young readers can also discuss the power of humor to overcome obstacles.

Chapman, Carol. *Herbie's Troubles*. New York: E. P. Dutton, 1981.
After trying the advice of each of his friends on how to deal with a bully, Herbie solves the problem himself: he cuts off the bully's fun by simply ignoring him. No adults ever get involved in this story. The listening and reading audience should derive satisfaction from this cleverly illustrated tale about a triumph over adversity.

Keats, Ezra Jack. *Goggles!* New York: Macmillan, 1969.
This story is encouraging for small children troubled by bullies. It acknowledges their fear and suggests a solution.

Robinson, Nancy Konheim. *Wendy and the Bullies*. New York: Hastings House Publishers, 1980.
A young girl is tormented by several children in her neighborhood and school and is too terrorized to ask for help. A talk with her parents strengthens her, and an assertive confrontation with each of her two chief enemies restores some of her self-esteem. The dialogue in this story rings true, and the relationship between the parents and child is nicely drawn.

Hospitalization

Carris, Joan Davenport. *When the Boys Ran the House*. New York: J. B. Lippincott, 1982.
Three resourceful brothers take over housekeeping and child-care responsibilities during their mother's illness and their father's absence. They survive numerous mishaps, solve their problems themselves, and learn some practical skills in the process.

Greene, Carla. *Doctors and Nurses: What Do They Do?* New York: Harper & Row, 1963.
This book describes typical work procedures of a doctor and a nurse. The instruments they use, the nature of their work, and the way they help people are described. The book is helpful for stressing the friendliness of these caregivers.

Hogan, Paula Z. and Kirk Hogan. *The Hospital Scares Me*. Milwaukee: Raintree Publishers, 1980.
This reassuring, simple, but informative account of a little boy's surgery and hospital stay could help prepare children for a hospital visit. It might also be useful for describing the hospital experience of others. The child in the story is very clear about his feelings and observations, making him an engaging character. Large colorful illustrations add to the appeal.

Stein, Sara. *A Hospital Story* (An Open Family Book for Parents and Children Together). New York: Walker, 1974.
Five-year-old Jill is anxious about her scheduled tonsillectomy. Her experience in the hospital is described in large, realistic photographs. This book is designed for parents and children to use together.

Wolff, Angelika. *Mom, I Broke My Arm*. Scarsdale, N. Y.: Lion Books, 1969.
This book explains what happens when the doctor says you've broken a bone.

Self Confidence

Delton, Judy. *I Never Win!* Minneapolis: Carolrhoda Books, 1981.
A little boy's frustration at always losing translates into great success at the piano, since whenever Charlie loses at something, he practices the piano furiously. Thus, playing becomes more than just a way of releasing his anger. It becomes a means of discovering his own worth.

Schick, Eleanor. *Joey on His Own*. New York: Dial Books, 1982.
A little boy goes to the store for the first time by himself, completing his errand with resounding success. Simple, attractive illustrations follow Joey as he describes his progress towards self-assurance. This story will appeal to many children on the verge of this sort of independence.

Simon, Norma. *Nobody's Perfect, Not Even My Mother*. Niles, Ill.: Albert Whitman & Co., 1981.
A cast of ethnically and racially varied children and adults, many shown pursuing untraditional tasks and occupations, helps young readers understand that everyone is good at something and that even adults fall short of perfection.